For my mother, a champion of the imagination
—M.L.

For Alison and Leslie
—J.P.

RANDOM HOUSE 🏠 NEW YORK

Text copyright © 1996 by Mallory Loehr. Illustrations copyright © 1996 by Jan Palmer.
All rights reserved under International and Pan-American Copyright Conventions. Published in the United States
by Random House, Inc., New York, and simultaneously in Canada by Random House of Canada Limited, Toronto.

http://www.randomhouse.com/

Library of Congress Cataloging-in-Publication Data
Loehr, Mallory. The princess book / by Mallory Loehr ; illustrated by Jan Palmer.
p. cm. SUMMARY: Includes ideas and simple instructions for costumes, jewelry, fanciful feasts,
royal decorations, and other items for the little girl who dreams of being a princess.
ISBN 0-679-87950-1 (hardcover) 1. Handicraft—Juvenile literature. 2. Children—Costume—Juvenile literature.
3. Children's parties—Juvenile literature. 4. Princesses in art—Juvenile literature. [1. Handicraft. 2. Princesses.]
I. Palmer, Jan, ill. II. Title. TT171.L64 1996 745.5—dc20 95-42667
Printed in the United States of America 10 9 8 7 6 5 4 3 2 1

THE
PRINCESS BOOK

Every girl
can be a princess—
with princess parties, recipes,
costumes, and more!

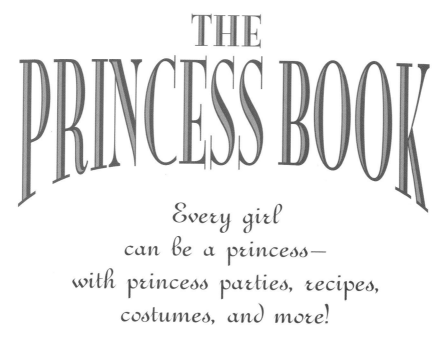

written by MALLORY LOEHR
illustrated by JAN PALMER

Dear Reader,

When I was a little girl, I loved to dress up as a princess and have marvelous adventures. For pretend balls and banquets, I wore a fancy dress with violet satin trim that my mother had made for me. Other times I would explore the neighborhood as Pocahontas, with my hair in braids and a headband around my forehead. And on still other occasions I would put on one of my mother's old gauzy nightgowns and dance around the garden, imagining that I was a fairy princess. It's a funny thing, though. While I loved pretending to be all these exotic princesses, my favorite princess wasn't really a princess at all. She was Sara Crewe, the heroine of Frances Hodgson Burnett's book *A Little Princess.*

Sara Crewe was not the daughter of a king or married to a prince—she was a princess in her heart, in her mind, and in her imagination. She made me see that being a princess is not about being rich and powerful or wearing the right clothes. A princess is a girl who is brave and kind, smart and creative, strong and fair. And if that's what being a princess is all about, then *all* girls can choose to be princesses, every day—whoever and wherever they are!

Mallory Loehr

Contents

8

Sleeping Beauty Slumber Party

When Princess Aurora fell asleep, so did everyone else in the castle.
The King and Queen fell asleep on their thrones, the cooks fell asleep over their
pots and pans, and the lords and ladies fell asleep in the courtyards and chambers.
Even the animals out in the stables fell asleep.

Time for bed! Invite a bunch of your best friends over for a Sleeping Beauty Slumber Party. Treat yourselves to a scrumptious fairy tale snack. Make pillowcases suitable for a slew of sleepy princesses, and dress up in your fanciest nightgowns or pajamas.

SLEEPING BEAUTY SLUMBER PARTY INVITATION:

You will need:

construction paper	*pencils*	*felt-tip pens*	*glue*
ribbons	*lace*	*scissors*	*glitter*

Fold a piece of construction paper in half. Draw the outline of a canopy bed on the front. Cut out a piece of the front of the card so that you see through to the inside, like this:

Glue a different-colored piece of paper to the inside of the card. Close the card and write "You are invited to a Sleeping Beauty Slumber Party!" the way it is shown in the picture. Open the card again and list all the information your guests need. Be sure to include:

• Your "princess" name and phone number.
• What guests should bring: their favorite nightgown or pajamas, a plain pillowcase, and a sleeping bag.
• When, where, and at what time the party will take place.
• RSVP. (This means that your friends should call to tell you whether or not they are coming to the party.)

Now use colored pens to decorate the cards. You can also add glitter, ribbons, and lace.

When you're done, either mail the cards or give them right to your friends. Then wait for everyone to RSVP!

SLEEPING BEAUTY BOWER

Sleeping Beauty slept for a hundred years. You only have to sleep for one night at a time. But every princess should sleep surrounded by beautiful things. Try making some of these decorations to create your own enchanted sleeping bower:

• Attach pastel-colored ribbons or crepe-paper streamers to the frame of the door to your room, using tape. Your guests will feel as if they're entering a secret, magical spot!
• Tape crepe-paper streamers to the walls of your room. Cover the tape with gold and silver star stickers.
• Tie back your curtains with colorful ribbons. Fasten small bells to the end of the ribbons.
• Arrange flowers around your room—they can be fresh or dried.

- If you have a four-poster bed, you can make a simple but elegant canopy. Just drape a pretty sheet over the bedposts and tie it in place with ribbons.
- Make the silver and gold decorations described on page 43.

SWEET DREAM SNACK

Ask a grown-up to help you make homemade hot chocolate and Sweet Dreams (or s'mores). For hot chocolate, follow the directions on a container of cocoa powder. Add a few marshmallows—or a dollop of whipped cream—to each mug to make this warm drink extra yummy.

Create your own Sweet Dreams by placing a slab of nut-filled chocolate and two marshmallows between two graham crackers. Put the sandwich on top of a paper towel in a microwave oven. Microwave on "high" for forty seconds or until the marshmallow is slightly melted. Sweet Dreams are best eaten while they're still warm. But be careful not to burn your tongue!

PRINCESS PILLOWS

Slumber sweetly on a luxurious pillow trimmed with ribbons and lace.
You will need:

plain pillowcase	*scissors*	*pins*
needle and thread	*ribbons*	*lace*

Ask an adult to help you. First pin on the lace and ribbons to help you figure out how to decorate your pillowcase. You may want to create a design on the front, or you may just want to decorate the ends. Trim the lace and ribbons to fit.

Thread the needle and make a knot in one end. Now sew the lace and ribbon onto the pillow with either a running stitch or a whipstitch:

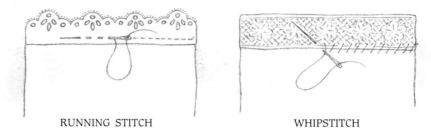

RUNNING STITCH   WHIPSTITCH

Sewing tips:
• Use fairly short pieces of thread; long pieces will tangle too easily.
• Make sure that your pillowcase is comfortable enough to sleep on!
• Be careful not to sew the top and bottom of the pillowcase together.

TALES TO TELL

What's a slumber party without stories? And what's a Sleeping Beauty Slumber Party without some royal stories? Here are some ideas to get you started:
• Tell each other your favorite fairy tales.
• Make up new fairy tales together. One person starts with "Once upon a time…" and each person adds a sentence until you've finished the story!
• Make up a fairy tale with a new twist—like a story about the handsome *prince* who slept for a hundred years!
• Tell a story about what happens *after* "happily ever after."

Here's another dreamy idea:

A PRINCESS AND THE PEA SLUMBER PARTY

All the princesses put dried peas under their pillows or mattresses before they go to sleep. In the morning, find out if anyone felt the pea. (With luck, no one is *that* sensitive!)

Princess Pocahontas Powwow

The princess Pocahontas knelt and covered John Smith's head with her own.
"Spare his life!" she cried to her father, the great chief Powhatan.
And so John Smith's life was spared and he was accepted by the tribe.

Over the years, the story of Pocahontas has grown into a legend. And like all legends, it is partly true and partly make-believe. Here are some facts that we know: Pocahontas was the daughter of Powhatan, a powerful Algonquin chief. John Smith and other settlers arrived in Powhatan's territory (now part of Virginia) in 1607, when Pocahontas was about eleven years old. John Smith was brought before Powhatan as a captive, and Pocahontas did shield his head to save his life. Why did she do it? We don't know for sure. The answer is found only in legend, where Pocahontas lives on—a true American princess!

PAINTED FACES

John Smith often visited Pocahontas's village. Sometimes Pocahontas and her friends
would paint their faces in his honor and perform a special dance.

You can celebrate in the same way! Buy nontoxic face-painting makeup. Paint different designs on your face—white for peace, blue for sky, red for life, and yellow for happiness. Then make up a dance to celebrate any occasion: a visit, a birthday, or simply a beautiful day. Most face paint comes off with cold cream, followed by soap and water.

ROASTED PUMPKIN SEEDS

Try out this recipe when you carve your Halloween pumpkin. Ask an adult to help you. Scoop the seeds out of the pumpkin. Spread the seeds out to dry on a tinfoil-lined cookie sheet.

Put the dry seeds in a bowl and add a tablespoon of vegetable oil. Stir them until all the seeds are coated with oil. (Add another tablespoon or so of oil if there are lots of seeds.)

Spread the seeds on a fresh piece of tinfoil on top of the cookie sheet. Sprinkle a little salt over them. Bake the seeds in the oven at 250°F until they're brown. Take them out of the oven and allow them to cool. Serve this crunchy treat in a basket lined with a decorative napkin or paper towel.

CORNCOB DOLL

Pocahontas probably played with corncob dolls that her mother or grandmother made for her. Make a corncob doll of your own and decorate it with things from nature, like seeds, dried flowers, and blades of grass.

Glue corn silk to the smaller end of a corncob for hair. Glue on seeds for the eyes and nose. Make a headband from a blade of grass. Sew a simple dress from scraps and decorate it with beads and feathers.

BEADS GALORE

Pocahontas made jewelry from beads. She also used beads to decorate clothing. She was especially fond of the glass beads that John Smith brought her. You can make beads from seeds, modeling dough, or paper. Or you can buy glass and plastic beads at a craft store.

String the beads together on fishing line, embroidery thread, yarn, or elastic to make necklaces, bracelets, anklets, and headbands. Try sewing beads in fancy patterns onto a vest, denim jacket, or jeans. You can also glue beads onto an old pair of shoes or an old belt.

SEED BEADS

Save watermelon seeds, pumpkin seeds, sunflower seeds, or corn kernels. Dry them on trays lined with paper towels.

Soften the seeds in a little bit of water. String the seeds together, using a needle and thread, or sew them onto a piece of clothing.

Tip: Use a thimble to protect your finger when pushing the needle through the seed.

DOUGH BEADS

To make the dough, combine ½ cup flour, ½ cup water, ¼ cup salt, 1 teaspoon vegetable oil, and 1 teaspoon cream of tartar. Double or triple the recipe, depending on how many beads you want to make.

Color the dough with food coloring, or paint the beads with poster paint after they're dry. Remember to poke holes in the beads with a pin or a nail *before* the beads dry. That way you'll be able to string them together. Make the beads in lots of different shapes.

PAPER BEADS

Cut a triangle out of a thin piece of paper. For a long bead, make the triangle about 2 inches long and 1 inch wide. For a shorter bead, make the triangle thinner. Roll up the piece of paper, starting at the base of the triangle. Tape or glue down the point of the triangle to complete your bead.

Practice making beads of all different shapes and sizes. Try using colorful, glossy magazine pages or newspaper. You can also color the beads with poster paint or spray paint. To make a bead shiny, coat it with a thin layer of glue. Always leave enough room in the center of the bead for a needle and thread to fit through.

NOODLE BEADS

These are quick and easy beads! Use macaroni, ziti, or any noodle through which you can thread some yarn. Use noodles of different shapes. Try painting the noodles before stringing them. Noodles make fabulous necklaces and bracelets!

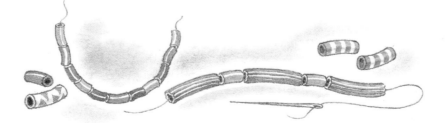

Cinderellas Around the World

Cinderella's eyes flew to the clock as it began to chime. It was midnight!
She pulled away from the Prince and ran through the ballroom and out the door.
The Prince followed her. On the palace steps lay a single glass slipper.
There was no sign of the lovely lady! The Prince picked up the dainty slipper.
"Whosoever's foot can fit this slipper shall be my bride," he vowed.

Cinderella stories are told the world over. The one many of us know best is the French tale told by Charles Perrault. But the oldest Cinderella stories are actually from Asia. The stories vary from country to country—and even within the same country. The fairy godmother is sometimes an old man, a fish, or even a giant frog! And the slipper is gold in China, rose-red in Egypt, and made out of fur in Russia.

A pair of magic slippers can transform you, like Cinderella, into a princess. Try making these different kinds of Cinderella Slippers. Just grab an old pair of shoes from the back of your closet—and remember to spread newspaper over your workspace to keep it clean!

GLASS SLIPPERS

Find clear, silver, or iridescent glitter at a craft store. Spread glue over an old pair of shoes. Sprinkle the glitter on and shake off any extra. Allow the glue to dry.

GOLDEN SLIPPERS

Yeh-Shen, a Chinese Cinderella, wore gold slippers and a cloak of feathers.

Ask an adult to help you paint an old pair of flip-flops with gold spray paint (follow the directions on the can). Allow the shoes to dry.

Spread glue along the straps of the flip-flops. Do the same thing on the edges of the soles. Sprinkle glitter on and allow it to dry.

FUR SLIPPERS

*In some Russian stories, Cinderella wore fur slippers—to keep warm
in the long Russian winter!*

Cut thin strips of fake fur. Carefully glue each one (with fabric glue) to an old pair of sneakers. Allow the glue to dry.

For quick and easy fur slippers, dig up a pair of old, furry bedroom slippers.

ROSE-RED SLIPPER

The tale of Rhodopis from Egypt is one of the oldest Cinderella stories.

Ask an adult to help you. Cut the backs off an old pair of sneakers so that your feet can easily slip into them. Cut thin strips of red satin or another shiny fabric. Glue the strips onto the sneakers one at a time, layering them until the whole shoe is covered. Wait for the glue to dry and then decorate with gold glitter fabric paint.

MORE CINDERELLAS

• In Scotland, Cinderella is called Ashenputtle because she sits among the ashes. The Scots also tell a tale of a boy Cinderella, called Assipattle!

• In India, a rich young man knows that he has found the real Cinderella (called Hanchi) when he tastes her rice dishes—no one else cooks the way she does!

• The Italian Cinderella, Rosina, doesn't find herself back in rags at midnight. Instead, she turns into a snake when a ray of sun hits her!

• Make up a Cinderella story of your own!

Moon Princess Magic

One bright night, a little basket sailed down a moonbeam—right into a bamboo grove
that stood beside the cottage of an old couple. Inside the basket
was something they'd been dreaming of...a beautiful baby girl!
She was wrapped from head to toe in moon-colored silk.

This traditional Japanese story tells of an old man and woman who pray to the moon for a child. In answer, the moon sends her own daughter down to earth. The Moon Princess lives as the old couple's daughter until their earthly days are over. Then she returns to her home in the heavens.

You, too, can be a Moon Princess. Dress up in a moon kimono and wear a moon blossom barrette in your hair. Then imagine what it would be like if *your* mother were the moon!

MOON KIMONO AND SASH

You will need:

old bathrobe	1 yard white shiny fabric	scissors
needle and thread	sequins, glitter, fake jewels	glue
glow-in-the-dark star stickers or fabric paint		

Decorate the edges of your bathrobe by gluing glitter, glow-in-the dark stars, sequins, and fake jewels onto the cuffs and hem. Look at some Japanese prints for inspiration—they often contain beautiful designs.

To make a sash, fold the piece of fabric in half lengthwise, shiny side in. Stitch along the long side and one short side, like this:

Turn the sash right side out. Ask a parent to help you iron the seams. Fold under the unstitched ends, iron them, and then sew them closed with small, neat stitches.

Put the sash on over the bathrobe and tie it in the back.

MOON BLOSSOM BARRETTE

You will need:

plain barrette	*1 yard ½-inch white ribbon*	*glue*
needle and thread	*scissors*	

Cut a section from the ribbon. The section should be a little longer than the barrette. Put this piece aside.

Now cut the remaining ribbon into three equal parts. With a needle and thread, sew a loose running stitch along the edge of one ribbon piece, like this:

When you have finished, slowly pull the thread and gather the ribbon. Hold the ribbon between your thumb and forefinger so that it curls around your finger as it is gathered. Do this until the ribbon is all curled. Now stitch it in place at the bottom to keep the flower-like shape. Make two more moon blossoms from the other two ribbon pieces.

Sew the three blossoms next to each other onto the small piece of ribbon you cut first. Glue the ribbon with the blossoms onto the barrette.

Make more moon blossoms and sew them onto your kimono!

Little Mermaid Pool Party

The Little Mermaid was the youngest daughter of the Mer-King. She understood the ocean tides and the language of the fish. She swam with the dolphins and made necklaces from pretty shells. And when she sang, she followed the rhythm and melody of the sea. But, oh, how the Little Mermaid longed to have human legs so that she could explore the vast land that lay beyond the sea.

It's funny that the Little Mermaid wanted with all her heart to be human; so many of us would love to trade places with her! You can create your own water world by throwing a *Little Mermaid Pool Party.* Choose a lovely warm day, invite friends over, and ask a grown-up or two to take you to a nearby pool, lake, or beach. You can also stay close to home and fill a baby pool, set up the sprinkler, or just turn on a hose for a little while.

MERMAID BANQUET

SEA-GREEN SALAD

Mix at least two different kinds of lettuce together in a large bowl. Now add your favorite green vegetables! Try green pepper, cucumber, avocado, watercress, or even dried seaweed! For more sea-lovin' fun, throw in little fish-shaped crackers (instead of croutons) and toss.

Pour on a green-colored salad dressing and dive in!

SWIMMING SANDWICHES

First, mix enough tuna fish salad to feed all of your guests. Then make regular tuna fish sandwiches. Cut each sandwich into diagonal halves. Place iceberg lettuce or *Sea-green Salad* in waves across your guests' plates. Arrange each sandwich in a fish shape on top of the lettuce bed. As the finishing touch, create a fishy eye from an olive or carrot slice!

For special starfish sandwiches, use a star-shaped cookie cutter to cut two slices of bread. Add tuna fish salad.

OCEAN LEMON-LIMEADE

With a grown-up's help, cut three lemons and three limes in half. Squeeze out the juice with a squeezer and then pour into a 2-quart pitcher. Add ½ cup of sugar. Fill the pitcher with water and stir. When the sugar is dissolved, add one drop of blue food coloring and one drop of green. Stir again. Slowly add more food coloring, stirring between drops, until the lemonade turns a pretty sea-green color.

Serve in tall glasses with ice and slices of limes. How refreshing!

FRUIT OF THE SEA

The perfect dessert for a *Mermaid Banquet!*

In a bowl, mix 4 cups of unsweetened grapefruit juice, ½ cup of sugar, and ½ cup of water. Once the sugar dissolves, pour the mixture into a shallow pan and put in the freezer for two hours. Give the mixture a quick stir every twenty minutes. When it's ready, spoon the mixture into bowls and serve. Yum!

UNDERWATER WONDERS

Have you ever noticed that the stones you find at the beach or in streams are never as pretty once they're dry? Well, here's a way to keep that shiny, wet look—simply put them back in the water!

Collect pretty, interesting, or unusual stones and pebbles. Put them into a clean jar. Fill the jar with water and put the top back on. The water will bring out the color in the stones and brighten up dull ones. You can make your *Underwater Wonder* even fancier by gluing a shell, sand dollar, or starfish to the top. Or tie a festive aqua ribbon around the neck of the jar. Then set the jar someplace where all your party guests will see it—but not near the pool. Glass and bare feet don't mix!

MERMAID JEWELRY

If you're near a beach, pick up shells there. Otherwise, you can usually find shells in craft stores, nature stores, or marine supply stores. Be sure to pick only those shells with holes in them.

To make a necklace: Cut a piece of string a few inches longer than you want your necklace to be. (Remember that you'll have to be able to slip it over your head.) Slide the shells one by one on to the string. You can make a simple necklace with one shell, or more complicated ones with large shells in the middle and smaller ones on either side. You can use shells of all one type or mix different sizes and colors.

When you're done, double-knot the ends of the necklace and put it on! For a different look, try stringing the shells on fishing line. Because the line is clear, the shells will look as if they're floating on you!

To make a shell crown: Follow the necklace directions, but use a piece of string or ribbon that fits around your head with a few inches to spare. When you're done, gently place the crown on your head. You can either wear it around your forehead or pin it in your hair.

POOL GAMES

• Mermaid Water Tag—This is a twist on the classic pool game *Marco Polo.* One "mermaid" is the sea witch, and she has to catch the other players while keeping her eyes closed. To find where the others are, she chants the word "little." The other players must respond with "mermaid!" The first swimmer the sea witch tags becomes the *next* sea witch.

• Sharks and Minnows—At the beginning of the game, one person is chosen as the "shark." All the other players are "minnows." The shark has to catch the minnows. Once a minnow is caught, she turns into a shark as well and helps the first shark catch the others. Each minnow becomes a shark until the very last minnow is caught. The first minnow to be caught becomes the first shark in the next game.

• Mermaid Races—Hold a pool race in which each "little mermaid" has to swim with her legs pressed together—mermaid-style!

WATER SAFETY

• Wait at least twenty minutes after eating to go swimming.

• Walk—don't run—near a swimming pool.

• Always wear sunscreen when you're in the sun.

• Listen to the lifeguard.

A Little Princess Hideaway

"If I am a princess in rags and tatters, I can be a princess inside.
It would be easy to be a princess if I were dressed in cloth of gold,
but it is a great deal more of a triumph to be one
all the time when no one knows it."

These are the words of Sara Crewe, the heroine of Frances Hodgson Burnett's classic story *A Little Princess*. Sara's wealthy, doting father brings her from India and settles her at a fancy London boarding school. When Mr. Crewe dies and the family fortune is lost, the nasty headmistress forces Sara to become a poor servant. But Sara learns that with the power of her imagination she can still be a Little Princess—because she is noble *inside*. Here are some of the things she did. Give them a try!

OPEN YOUR EYES

"You can see all sorts of things you can't see downstairs."

When Sara's friend Lottie visits her in the attic, she is horrified at the cold, bare garret room. But Sara points out the good things: the sky is closer, the smoke curls from the chimneys in lovely patterns, and the sparrows chatter to one another, just like little people!

Look out a window at home—what do you see? When you open your eyes in this special way, you'll be surprised at the beauty in the simple things all around you.

SECRET CODE

Sara and her friend Becky live in two little attic rooms right next to each other. Sometimes they pretend they are prisoners. Sara has made up a code so that they can talk to each other even when they're in their own rooms. Two knocks on the wall means "Prisoner, are you there?" Three knocks means "Yes, I am here, and all is well." Four knocks means "Then, fellow-sufferer, we will sleep in peace. Good night."

Make up a code or language that only you and your friends can understand. For example, try saying the opposite of what you mean, or knocking on the wall like Sara and Becky, or making up a sign language of hand signals.

You can also use a written code in which you substitute numbers for letters.

FROM RAGS TO RICHES

The room in her dream seemed changed into fairyland...

Sara woke up in her attic room one night to discover that Magic had happened! On her bed was a satin-covered down quilt. A fire blazed in the fireplace, and on a small table covered with a tablecloth stood platters of piping-hot, wonderful-smelling food. As the days passed, the Magic continued—and gradually the room became filled with all sorts of fascinating and beautiful things.

In *A Little Princess*, "the Magic" was worked by Sara Crewe's wealthy neighbor, who turned out to be Mr. Crewe's best friend! You can work your own magic almost anywhere—your attic, basement, garage, or even a tree house. Give your private space an exotic flair by decorating it with deep, rich colors.

WALL COVERINGS

Some odd materials of rich colors had been fastened against the wall...
brilliant fans were pinned up...

Cover any unattractive parts of the wall with pieces of fabric. Hang up pictures you've drawn, prints of famous paintings, pretty magazine pages, and photos of your family and friends.

SITTING CUSHIONS

...there were several large cushions, big and substantial enough to use as seats.

To make one sitting cushion, use two large dishcloths of the same size. Pin the cloths together. Sew around the dishcloths about an inch from the edge with embroidery thread, leaving open a 6-inch space for stuffing. Stuff the pillow with purchased stuffing or scraps of fabric. Sew up the opening.

Decorate your pillow with tassels at the corners or lace and fringe around the edges. Make several pillows, one for each of your friends to sit on.

AND MORE...

- Cover a mantel with a scarf or embroidered cloth.
- Drape a pretty scarf across a milk crate and use as a table.
- Paste pictures of things you love to the sides of an old bookcase.
- Add a tassel to a light cord.
- Create a makeshift sofa by covering an old trunk with a blanket or thin rug.
- Decorate an old lampshade by gluing lace or fringe around the top and bottom.

When you're all done, invite friends over for a snack and read *A Little Princess* together in your Magic place.

African Princess Finery

Long ago, a wise King announced that he was in search of a wife.
One man sent his two beautiful daughters, so the King could choose
which one was the more worthy of being Queen.
The King tested the two sisters by turning himself first into a beggar,
then an old woman, and finally a snake. One sister was haughty and cruel,
as she thought a Queen should be.
The other sister was thoughtful and generous to beggar and King alike.
The King knew that she was the Queen he had been looking for!

This story comes from Zimbabwe, Africa.

TIE-DYEING

The new Queen wore clothes woven by the finest weavers in the land.

Tie-dyeing gets its name from the fact that the cloth is first tied with string, or in knots, and then dyed. In many parts of Africa, the weaving and dyeing of cloth is an ancient and very important tradition. It is also quite complex. But you can do some simple tie-dyeing of your own and create gorgeous *African Princess Finery.*

You will need:

cotton T-shirt or a piece of cloth   *scissors*
string, yarn, or rubber bands   *packages of dye*

With an adult's help, follow the directions on the package for making cold dye.

Dyeing tips:

• Put each color of dye in a clean garbage can or bucket.

• You can buy inexpensive packages of men's undershirts—they're perfect for dyeing!

• Always use natural fabrics, such as cotton or silk.

• Get the cloth wet before putting it in the dye.

• Stir the cloth in the dye so that the color spreads itself evenly.

• Ironing the tie-dyed cloth (with an adult's help) after it has dried helps to set the color.

• Wash the dyed item separately or with other dark colors.

STRIPES AND LINES

This pattern is popular in Senegal and Gambia.

Lay the T-shirt flat. Fold it like a fan or accordion—horizontally, vertically, or diagonally. Tie in place. Dye.

MARBLING

Crumple the T-shirt up and tie it in a bundle. Dye.

BIG SPIRAL

Lay the T-shirt flat. Pinch the center of the shirt between your thumb and forefinger. Twist the cloth in a circle, so that it wraps around your fingers.

When the cloth is completely twisted, carefully hold it together and wrap with string. Dip half of the shirt into the dye for ten minutes or so.

For a two-colored spiral, dip the undyed half in a different-colored dye for ten minutes.

BIG CIRCLES, LITTLE CIRCLES

This pattern comes from Yorubaland, in Nigeria, and can also be called *Big Moons and Little Moons*.

Lay the T-shirt flat. Pinch a small section of the cloth between your thumb and forefinger and gather it into a knot. Tie in place, like this:

Repeat this all over the T-shirt. Dye.

TWISTED T

Twist the entire T-shirt tightly, as seen below. Tie it together with string. Dye.

TWO COLORS AND MORE

Follow the instructions for *Twisted T*. Dye the shirt or cloth in the darker color first. Untie the shirt and shake it out. Now dip it in the lighter dye. This will dye the white stripes (it may also change the color of the first dye slightly). For more colors, allow the T-shirt to dry a little and then use a paintbrush to apply fabric paint.

MIX IT UP

Try several of these methods together and see what you end up with!

MORE DYEING IDEAS:

• Experiment with tea as a dye. You should end up with an attractive light brown-colored fabric.

• Use fabric paints to create designs on a unicolored T-shirt.

• To inspire African Princess dreams, ask your parents if you can try tie-dyeing your sheets and pillowcases.

AFRICAN PRINCESS COSTUME

Dye a piece of cotton large enough to wrap around you one and a half times—an old trimmed sheet works well. Indigo (a deep blue) is very popular in many African countries, so you may want to dye your cloth blue.

To make a dress, wrap the cloth under your armpits and tuck under in the front. Use a safety pin to hold it in place. For a halter dress, bring the cloth around you and hold the ends out in front of you. Then twist the ends, cross them, and bring them up and around your neck. Tie in place. If your cloth is too big, trim it until your dress fits just right.

Make bright glass or plastic bead jewelry to go with your costume. Or make the beads from pages 15-17.

Fairy Princess Garden Party

Haven't you always wanted to peek into fairyland? And doesn't it seem as if all natural things have been touched by a fairy's magic wand—from acorns to roses, from fallen leaves to blades of fresh green grass? I still find myself looking for fairy rings and checking under mushrooms, thinking that if I am quick enough I might just catch sight of a fairy princess.

Always hold your *Fairy Princess Garden Party* outside—pick a local park for the location if you don't have any green space of your own. Invite your friends—but you can also host a fairy princess party all by yourself, with the flowers and trees as guests of honor. And remember to keep your eyes open...you never know when a <u>real</u> fairy princess might invite herself into your life!

FAIRY FROZEN FRUIT FEAST

A fairy feast is as tiny as a human's snack—so plan on eating dinner later!

ORANGE FROST

Ask an adult to help you cut four thin-skinned oranges into six wedges each. Peel the skin off halfway. Curl the peel under and secure with a toothpick. Arrange the wedges on a baking sheet and put in the freezer for one hour. Serve on little fairy-sized plates.

FROZEN CHOCOLATE BANANA

Peel the skin off of several bananas. Poke a Popsicle stick though the bottom of each banana. (Unripe bananas work best.) Place the bananas on a tinfoil-lined cookie sheet.

Pour chocolate syrup or fudge sauce over the bananas. Put the tray in the freezer until the chocolate hardens.

FRUIT GEMS

Put 5 ice cubes in a blender. Add ½ cup of fruit juice (or ¼ cup of one juice, ¼ cup of another), 2 tablespoons of cream of coconut, and ½ cup of chopped fruit. With an adult's help, blend on "high" until smooth. Pour into two glasses and garnish with slices of fruit. It's a treat fit for a fairy princess!

Try these fruity combinations or make up some of your own:
- orange juice with bananas, strawberries, and plums
- grapefruit juice with nectarines and bananas
- pineapple juice with peaches and watermelon
- pink lemonade with oranges and grapefruit
- orange/pineapple juice with grapes, bananas, and peaches

BUBBLE BLISS

Pour 2 tablespoons of dishwashing liquid into a large jar. Add 2 cups of hot water. Put the top on the jar and shake well. To make extra-strong bubbles, let the mixture stand for a few hours—then add a couple of pinches of sugar and stir until the sugar is dissolved. Now you're ready to blow!

Either use an old bubble wand, buy one, or make a wand by bending and twisting a piece of thin wire into a circle.

For super-big bubbles, make a double batch of bubble mixture. Pour it into a shallow pan. Cut a piece of string 12 inches long. Tie the ends together. Tightly hold the string between the thumb and forefinger of each hand and dip the string into the bubble mix. Simply blow at the string, or else hold it above your head and bring it down with a smooth, quick motion so that it fills with air and makes a bubble. Try different sizes of string and different ways of holding it.

FAIRY WAND

You will need:

a dowel at least 18 inches long (½ inch to 1 inch in diameter)
¼ yard shiny material
needle and thread (same color as fabric)
glitter and glue   long ribbons

a sheet of posterboard
scissors   pins
stuffing   newspaper

Ask an adult to help you cut a five-pointed star out of posterboard, about 6 inches wide and tall. This is your pattern.

Fold the material in half, with the shiny side in. Pin your pattern to the material and cut around it. Remove the pattern piece and pin the star together (shiny side still in).

Sew around the star, a half inch from the edges. Leave the bottom open.

Turn the star right side out. Fill the star with stuffing. Whipstitch around the unsewn bottom edges, leaving a small hole about half an inch long.

Apply a little glue to one end of the dowel. Attach the star to the dowel by pushing the dowel through the stuffing at the opening of the star. Glue the star and dowel together where they meet.

Wrap a long ribbon around the star and dowel, as shown. Tie at the end. Tie more ribbons up at the top, leaving the ends dangling. Put a little glitter on the star points for a touch of fairy dust!

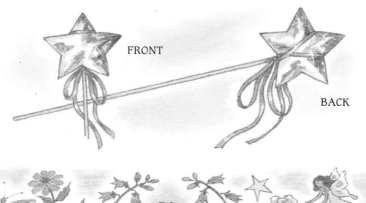

FRONT

BACK

FAIRY WINGS

You will need:

a sheet of posterboard   *2-inch-wide ribbon*   *scissors*

Fold the posterboard in half lengthwise. Draw a wing shape on it, like this:

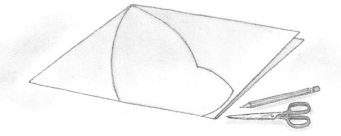

Ask an adult to help you cut out the wings and open them flat. Decorate them any way you want. You can even glue feathers on them!

When you have finished, cut out small holes above and below where your shoulders will be when you put the wings on. Thread the ribbons through the top holes and bottom holes. Tie the wings around your shoulders and wave your magic wand. You've been transformed into a fairy princess!

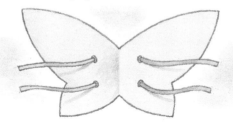

RAINBOW TREASURE BOX

Every fairy princess needs one to hold her natural treasures.

You will need:

a light-colored cardboard box (such as a shoe box)   *colored tissue paper*
glue   *paintbrush*   *small plate*
cup of water   *newspaper*

Spread the newspaper out where you'll be working. Tear the tissue paper into medium-sized strips. Pour a little bit of glue on the plate and thin with a few drops of water. Stir with the paintbrush.

Turn the box over so that the bottom faces up. Use the paintbrush to spread a thin layer of the glue-and-water mixture onto about a quarter of the box bottom. Lay a tissue strip on top of the glue. Smooth it down with the paintbrush and a little glue. Add another strip of tissue and do the same. It's okay to layer the pieces of tissue. When you've finished with that quarter of the box, spread a thin layer of glue over another quarter. If a piece overlaps the side of the box, simply glue it in place.

After you've done the bottom of the box, move to the sides (keeping the box upside down). Once the sides are finished, let the glue dry and go on to the box top. Glue the tissue on the same way and then let it dry.

You can also tissue-paper the inside of the box (after the outside is dry).

FLOWER WREATH AND CHAIN

Collect daisies or wildflowers, keeping the stems long.
Make a small slit at the end of a stem, like this:

Slide a second flower stem through the first. Make a small slit in the second stem and slide a third flower in. Continue until you have a "chain" long enough to go around your head. Tie the last stem right below the head of the first flower.

You can also make gorgeous garlands, necklaces, rings, and bracelets this way.

FAIRY FICTIONS

If you want to discover more about fairy princesses, fairies, and the wonders of fairyland, read some of these classic stories:

- *Thumbelina*, by Hans Christian Andersen
- The Flower Fairies Books, by Cicely Mary Barker
- *Peter Pan,* by J. M. Barrie
- The colored Fairy books, by Andrew Lang
- *A Midsummer Night's Dream*, a play by William Shakespeare

Twelve Dancing Princesses Dress-up Ball

Every night the King locked his twelve daughters into their bedroom.
But every morning the silk and satin shoes of the Princesses were completely worn out.
No one could guess where the Princesses went...until one night a brave young gardener
discovered their secret—the Princesses had been put under a spell! Every night they
traveled to an underground castle and danced at an enchanted ball.

For your own fairy tale ball, turn your living room—or bedroom—into an elegant ballroom. Invite all your Princess and Prince friends and put on some good dancing music. You don't have to be under a spell to have a ball!

GOLD AND SILVER DECORATIONS

On their nightly journey to the underground castle, the Princesses traveled through forests of gold, silver, and diamonds.

You will need:

sticks or tree branches, with or without leaves   *white Christmas tree lights*
nontoxic gold and silver spray paint   *glue*
newspaper   *glitter*

Collect long sticks and branches. To make the diamond branches, strip any leaves off the branches. Then ask a grown-up to help you weave white lights around the branches and plug the lights in.

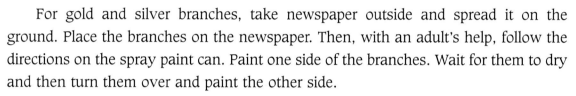

For gold and silver branches, take newspaper outside and spread it on the ground. Place the branches on the newspaper. Then, with an adult's help, follow the directions on the spray paint can. Paint one side of the branches. Wait for them to dry and then turn them over and paint the other side.

Once the branches are completely dry, you may want to glue glitter on them. Or you can leave them plain. Arrange them in vases. You can also tie a bunch of branches together with shiny ribbons and hang them on your wall. Dried flowers make an extra-fancy touch!

Dress up like a princess in a long, flowing skirt and lots of jewels. Then try making these costume accessories:

PRINCESS HATS

You will need:

a sheet of posterboard   *old scarves or scraps of material*   *1 yard of fabric*
fabric glue   *stapler or masking tape*
optional: ribbons, glitter, glue, fake fur

Roll the posterboard into a cone. Leaving a small hole at the point, tape the edges together with a small piece of tape. Put the cone on your head and ask someone to help you adjust it by moving the tape and tightening or loosening the cone. If the cone comes down too far over your forehead, draw a line on the posterboard where you need to trim it.

Ask an adult to help you cut. Untape the cone and cut along the line, if you've made one. Next, place the cone on top of the piece of fabric. Cut around the edges of the posterboard, leaving an inch on each side. Spread fabric glue on the posterboard, leaving about two inches unglued on each side. Roll the posterboard into a cone again, leaving a small hole at the point. Firmly tape in place both on the inside and outside. Glue the fabric to the cone. Turn the loose bottom edge of fabric under and glue in place.

Tie a knot in one end of a scarf or scrap of material. Put the other end of the scarf inside the hat and thread it through the hole in the top. Pull the scarf through. The knot inside should hold it in place. Dress up your hat with ribbons, glitter, and fake fur.

GLAMOUR GLOVES

Sew ribbons around the bottom edges of an old pair of gloves with a loose stitch. You can leave the ends of the ribbons dangling or you can tie them in bows. Put on the gloves. Now carefully glue the plastic jewels in place on your fingers, as shown. Or you can dab a little glue on the gloves and add glitter. Allow the glue to dry.

ROYAL LIMBO

The limbo is a dance contest that began in the West Indies. To do the limbo, all you need is a broom, some space, and good music. You can make your broom more regal by tying ribbons around it.

Two people hold either end of the broom at shoulder height. All the guests line up and dance under the broom one by one, bending backward. After everybody has gone under, the broom is lowered a little. If someone can't get under the broom, or falls down, he or she is out of the contest. The broom is lowered further and further each time around until only one person is left—the winner!

ORANGE BLOSSOM MAGIC POTION

The Twelve Dancing Princesses served a sweet magic potion to the Princes who tried to guess their secret. The potion made the Princes fall asleep. Prepare this "magic" potion. It won't make you sleepy, but it *will* quench your thirst!

Pour equal amounts of orange soda and orange juice into a punch bowl. Add orange slices and scoops of orange sherbet. Serve in paper cups (or punch cups) and keep spoons handy for the sherbet.